ELMO'S First Babysitter

Published by Creative Edge, 2010, an imprint of Dalmatian Publishing Group, Franklin, Tennessee 37067. No part of this
book may be reproduced or copied in any form without written permission from the copyright owner. 1-800-815-8696

Printed in China

CE12917/0410/ZHE

Elmo is so excited! Elmo is going to have a babysitter tonight! Her name is Emily. There's the doorbell! That must be Emily!

Um, wait a minute. Maybe Elmo doesn't really want a babysitter after all.

It *is* Emily. She looks nice, doesn't she? Elmo's mommy and daddy wrote down the phone number of the place they're going tonight. And they also wrote the phone numbers of our neighbors, just in case. Now it's time to hug Mommy and Daddy good-bye.

Sweetheart, you're going to have fun with Emily!
We'll come kiss you good night when we get home.
Mommy! Daddy! Are you sure you really want to go?

Did you see what we made? Kooky faces! Elmo made this one all by himself!

Wow! Elmo likes this music!

Elmo's toe feels all better now. And look—Emily brought
bubbles for Elmo to play with in the bathtub. When Mommy and
Daddy give Elmo a bath, we don't ever get to blow bubbles.

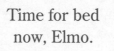

Time for bed now, Elmo.

Elmo's daddy always tells a story at bedtime. Could you please tell Elmo a story?

Emily told Elmo a story he'd never heard, called "The Brave Little Monster."

Good night, Elmo.
Good night, Emily. Elmo will stay awake until Mommy and Daddy come home.
Okay, Elmo. I'll be in the living room if you need me.

Good morning, Mommy! Good morning, Daddy!
Elmo liked having a babysitter! It was fun!
When is Emily coming back?